Ready for Lift Off

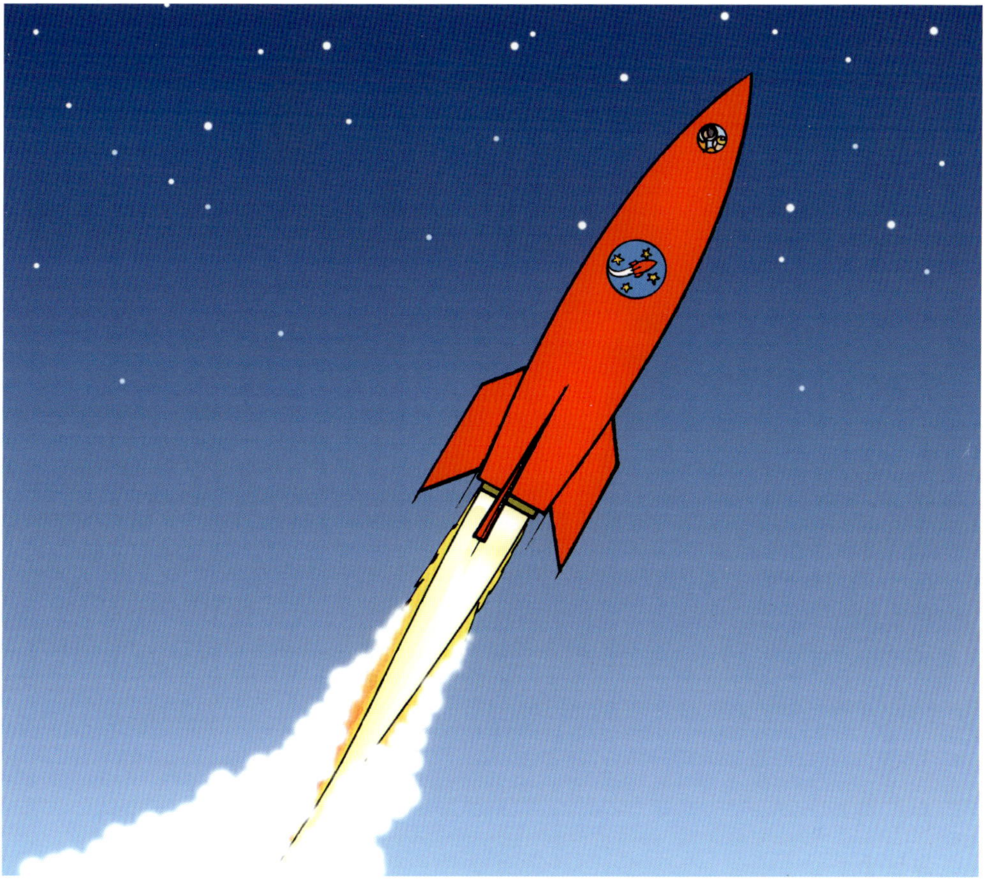

written by Rachel Walker
illustrated by Robin Van't Hof

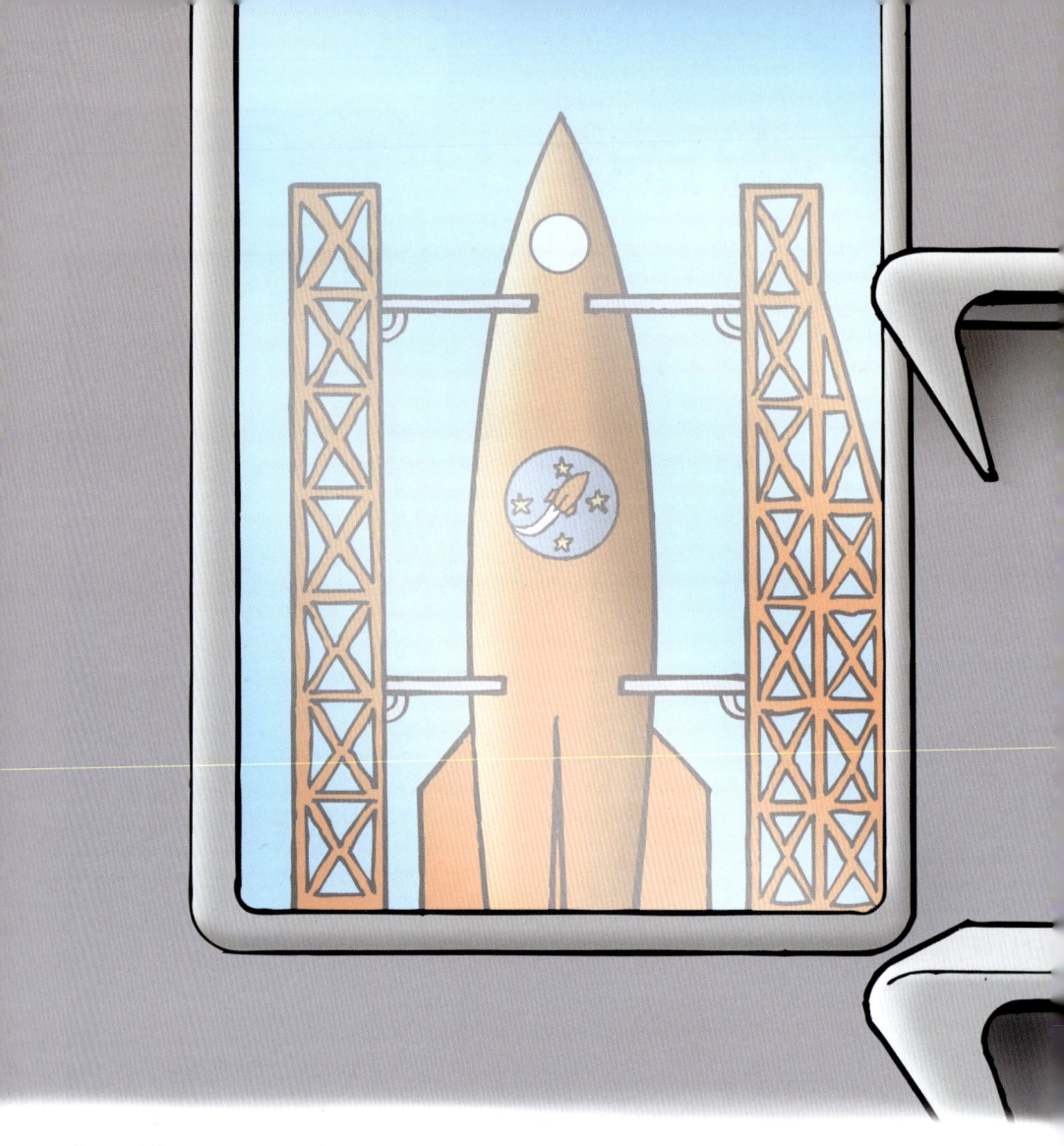

We put on
our space suits.

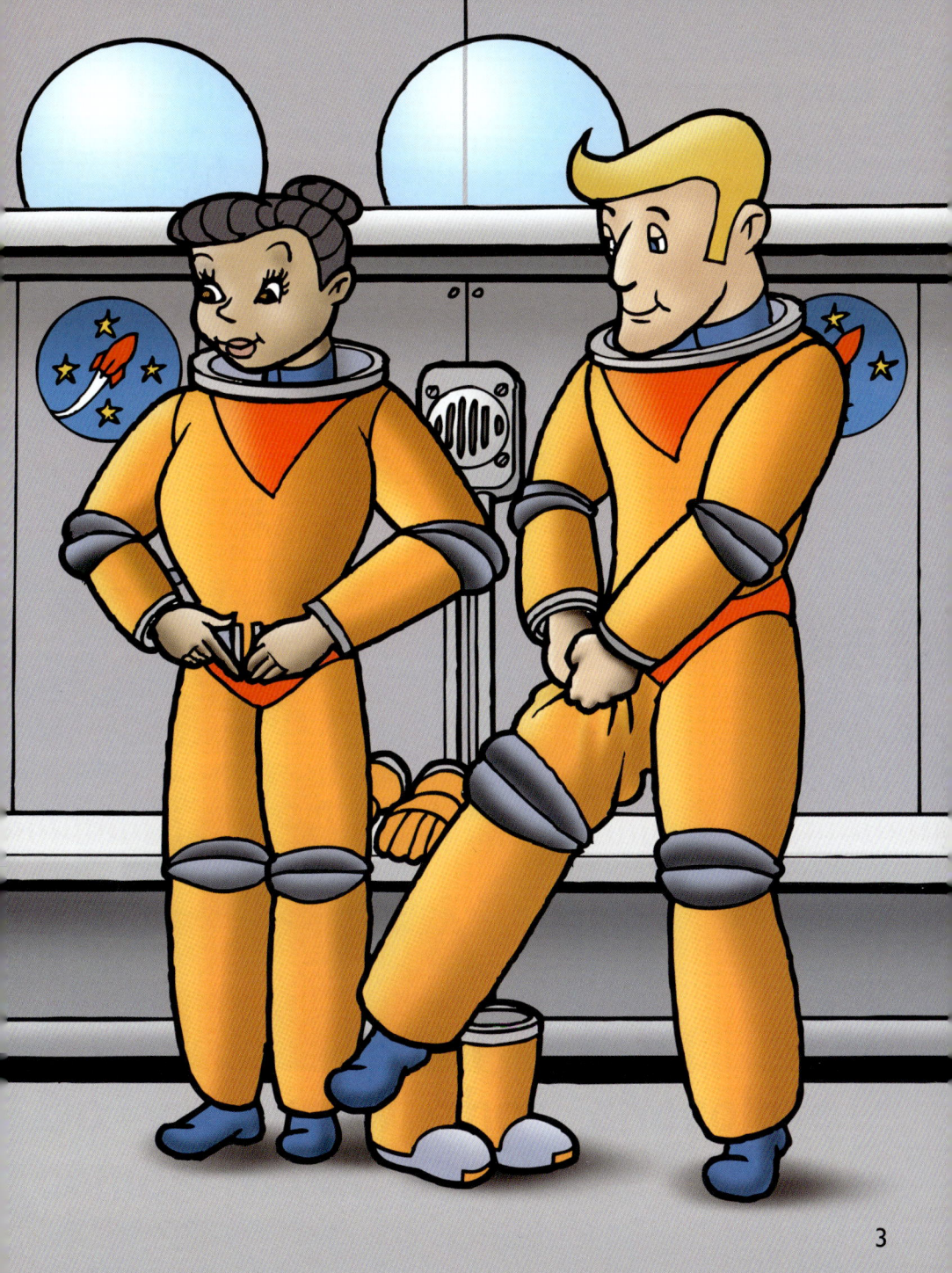

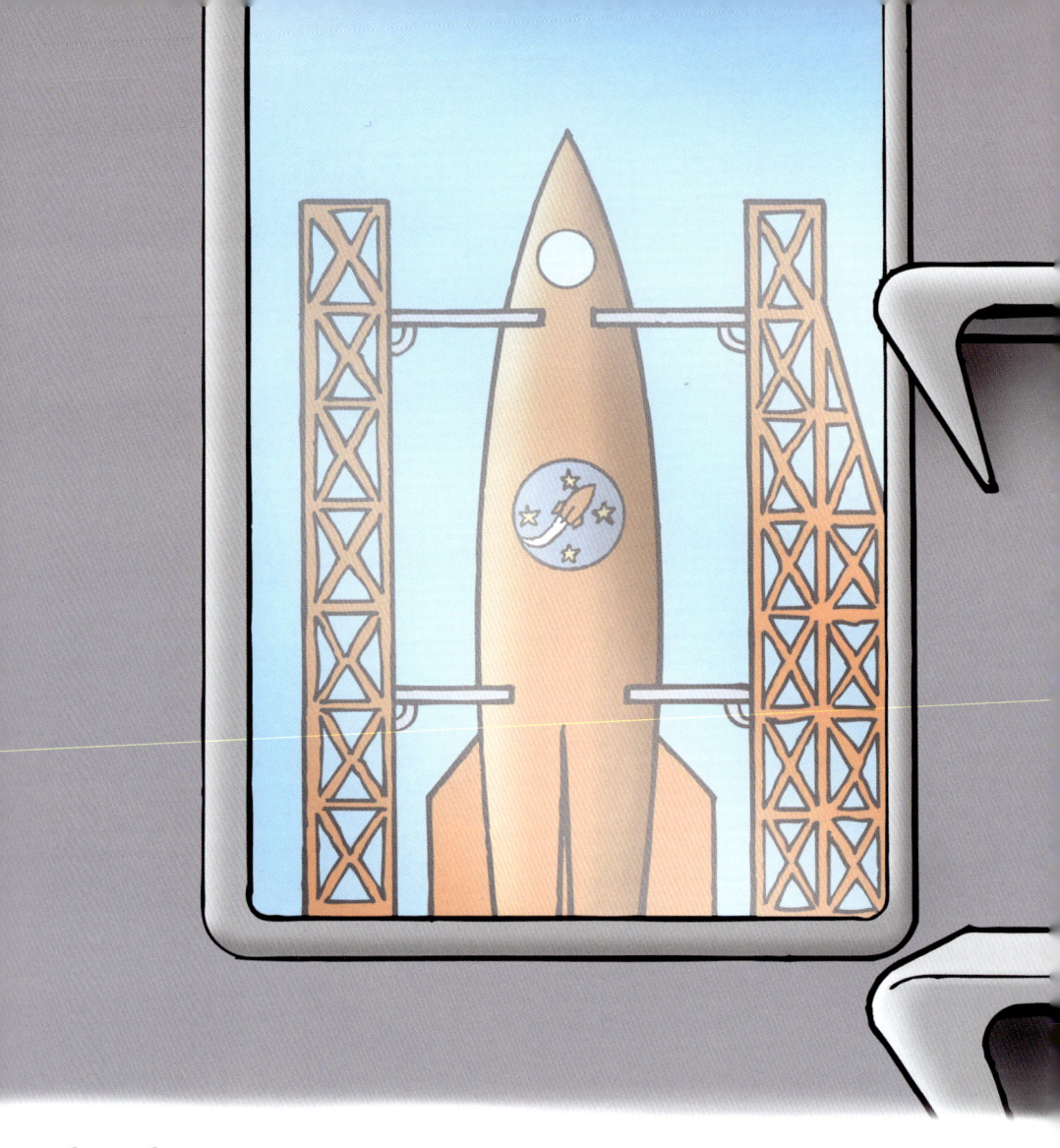

We put on
our helmets.

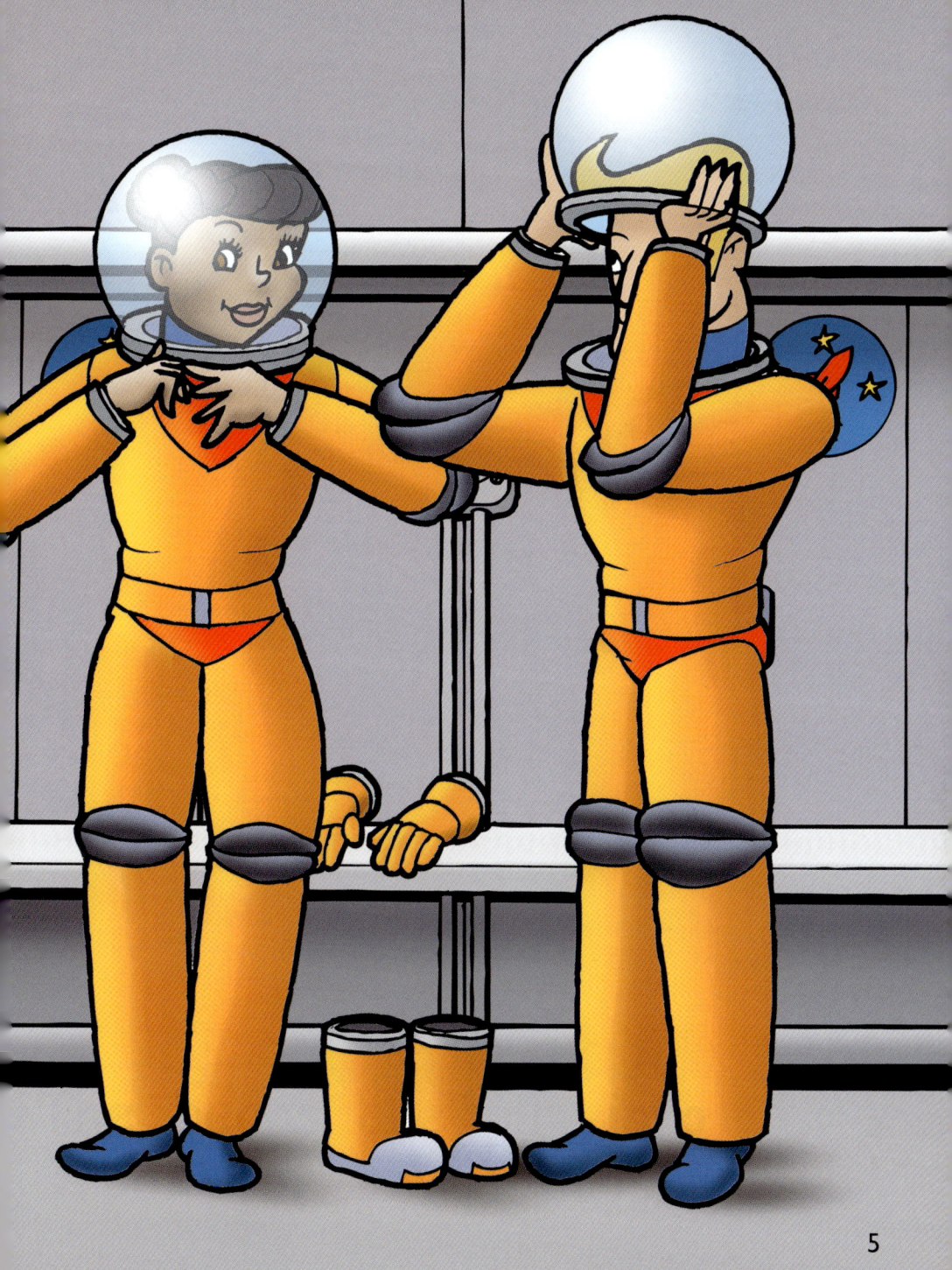

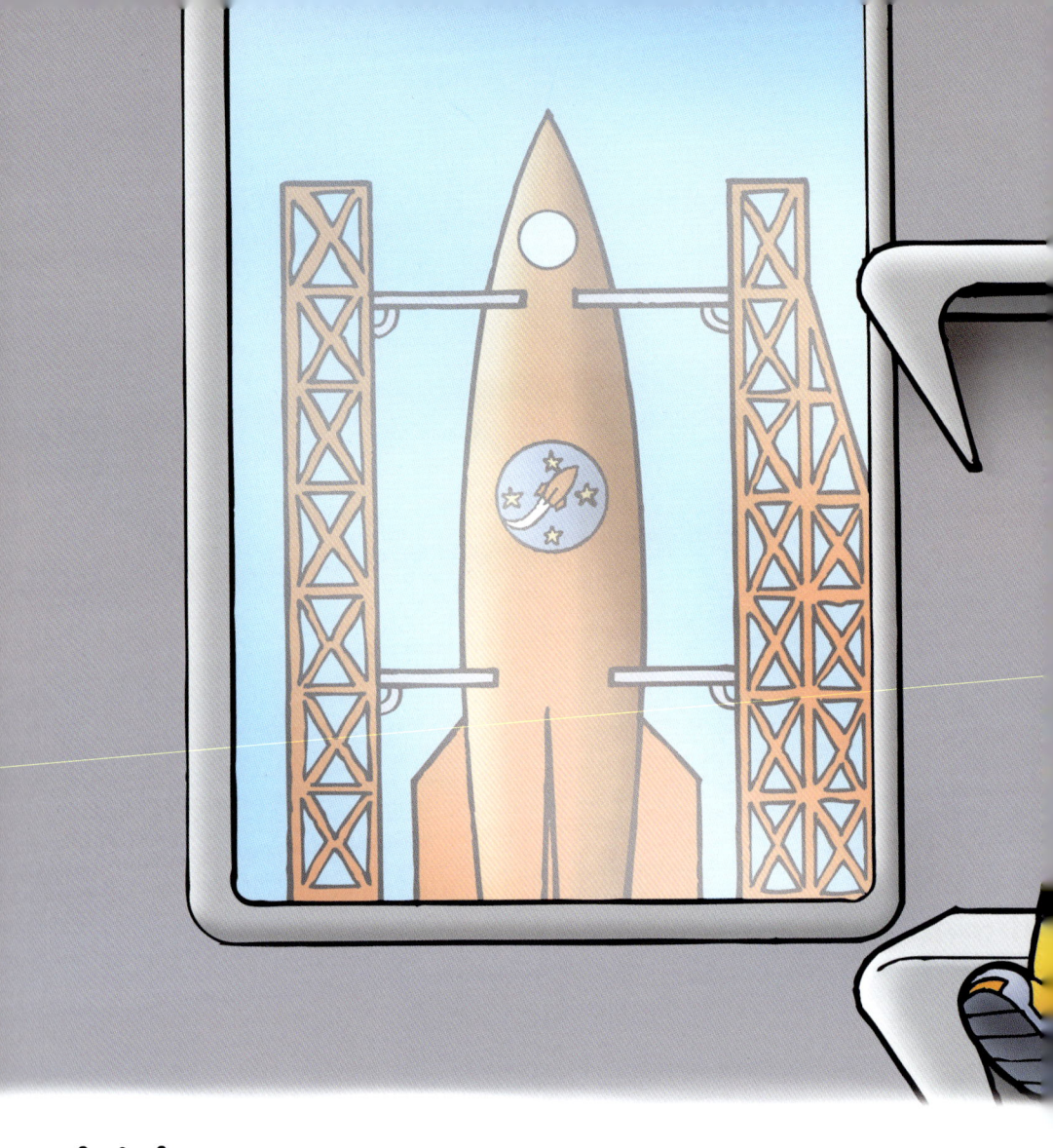

We put on
our boots.

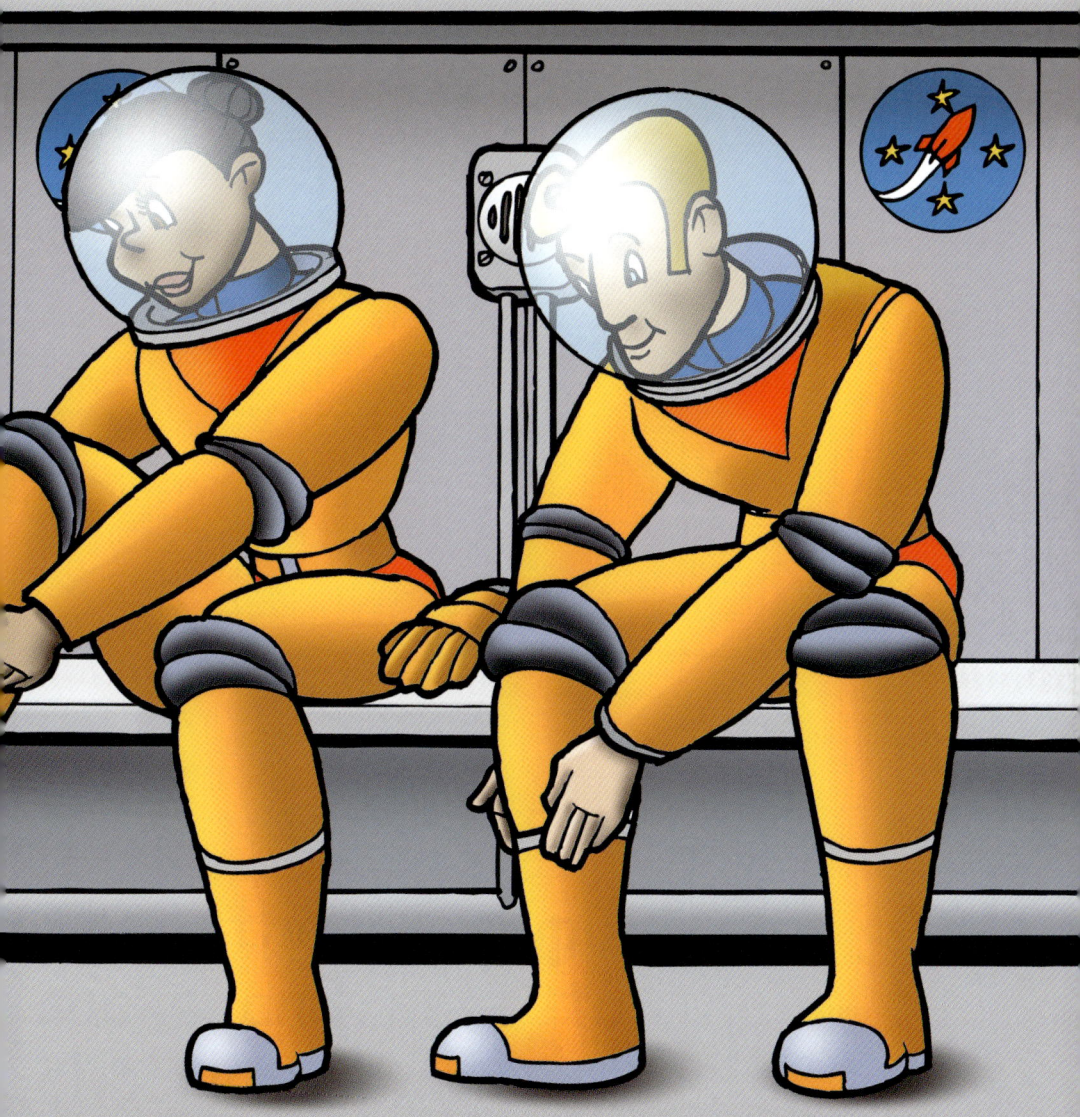

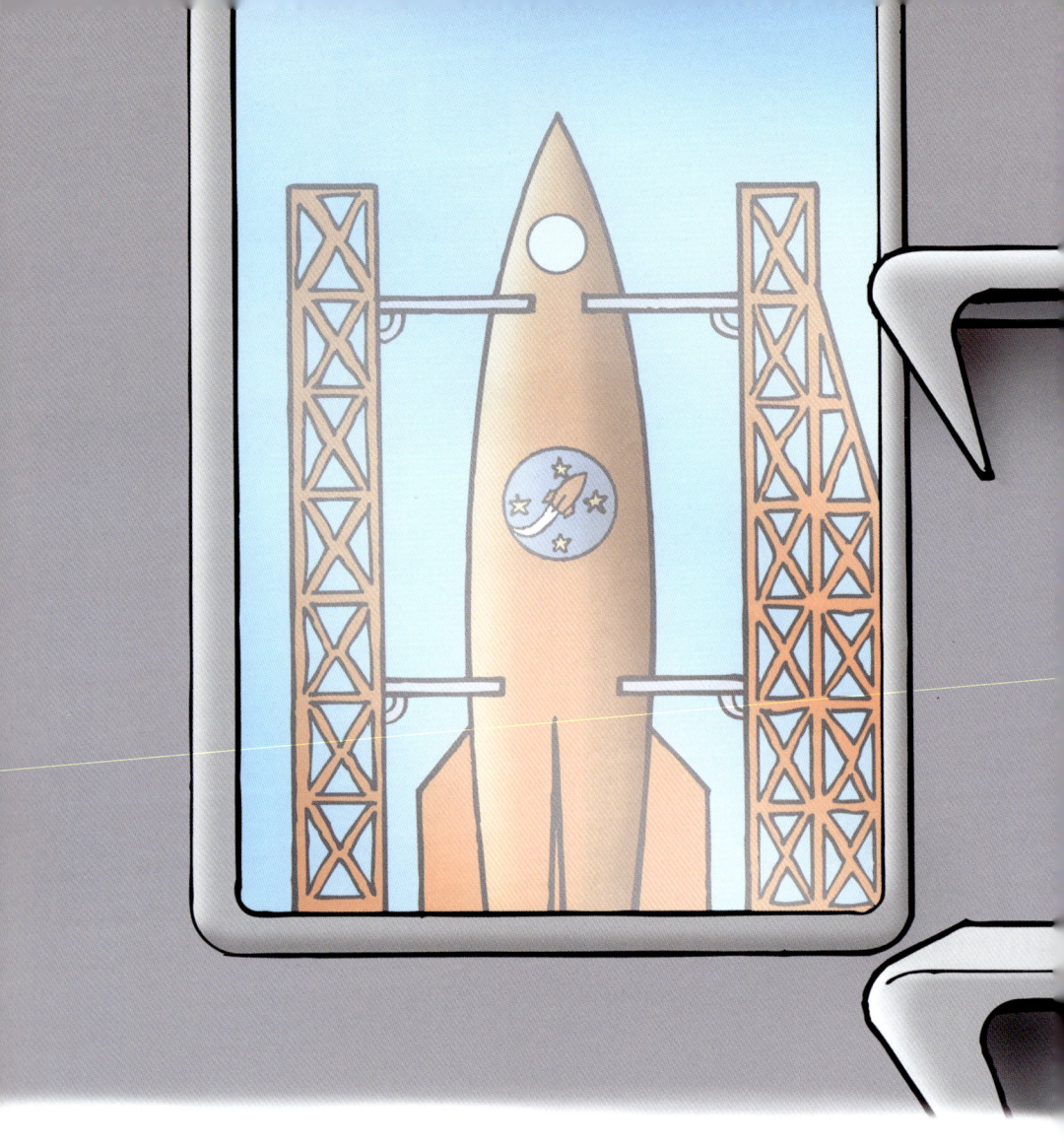

We put on
our gloves.

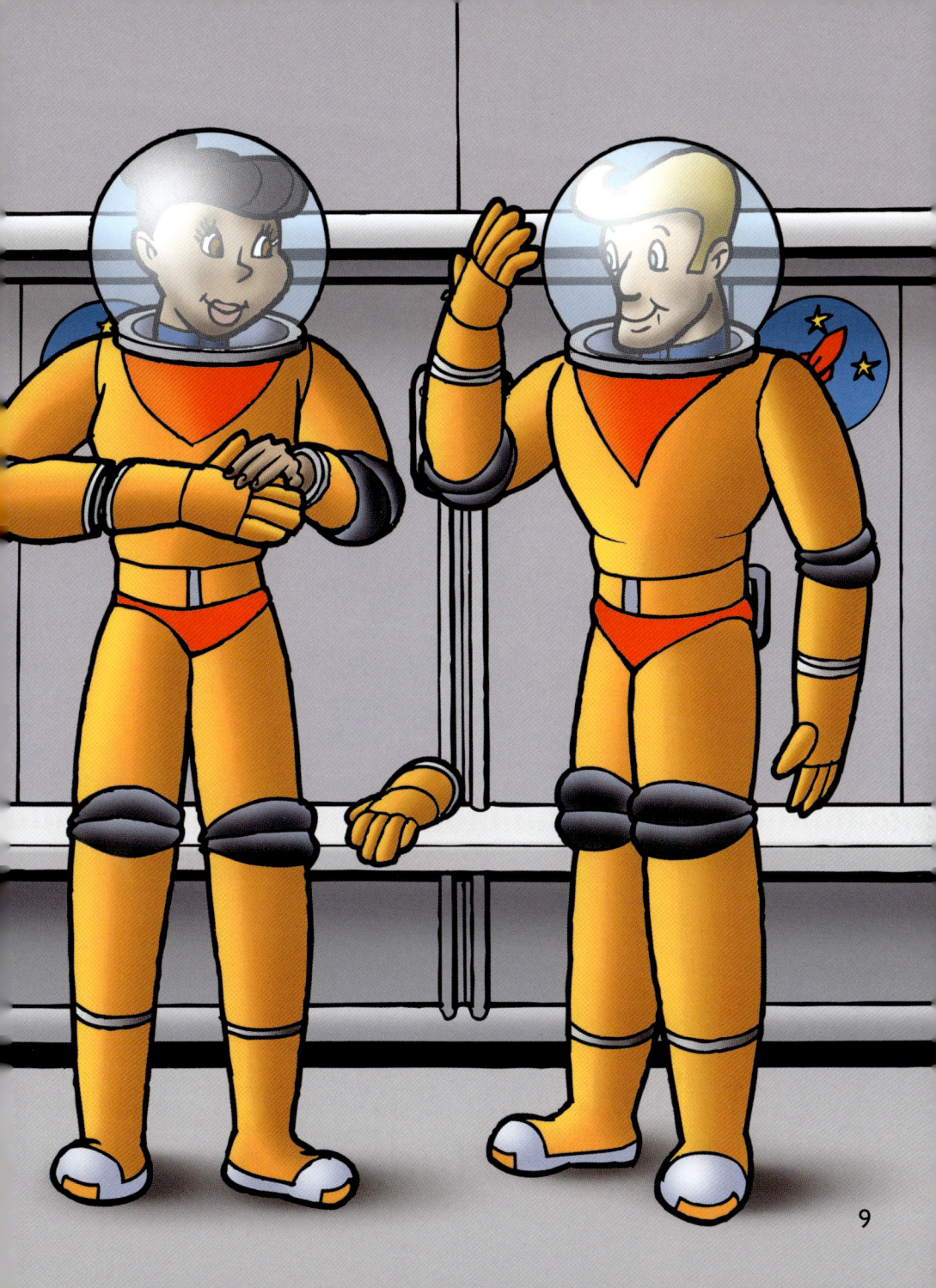

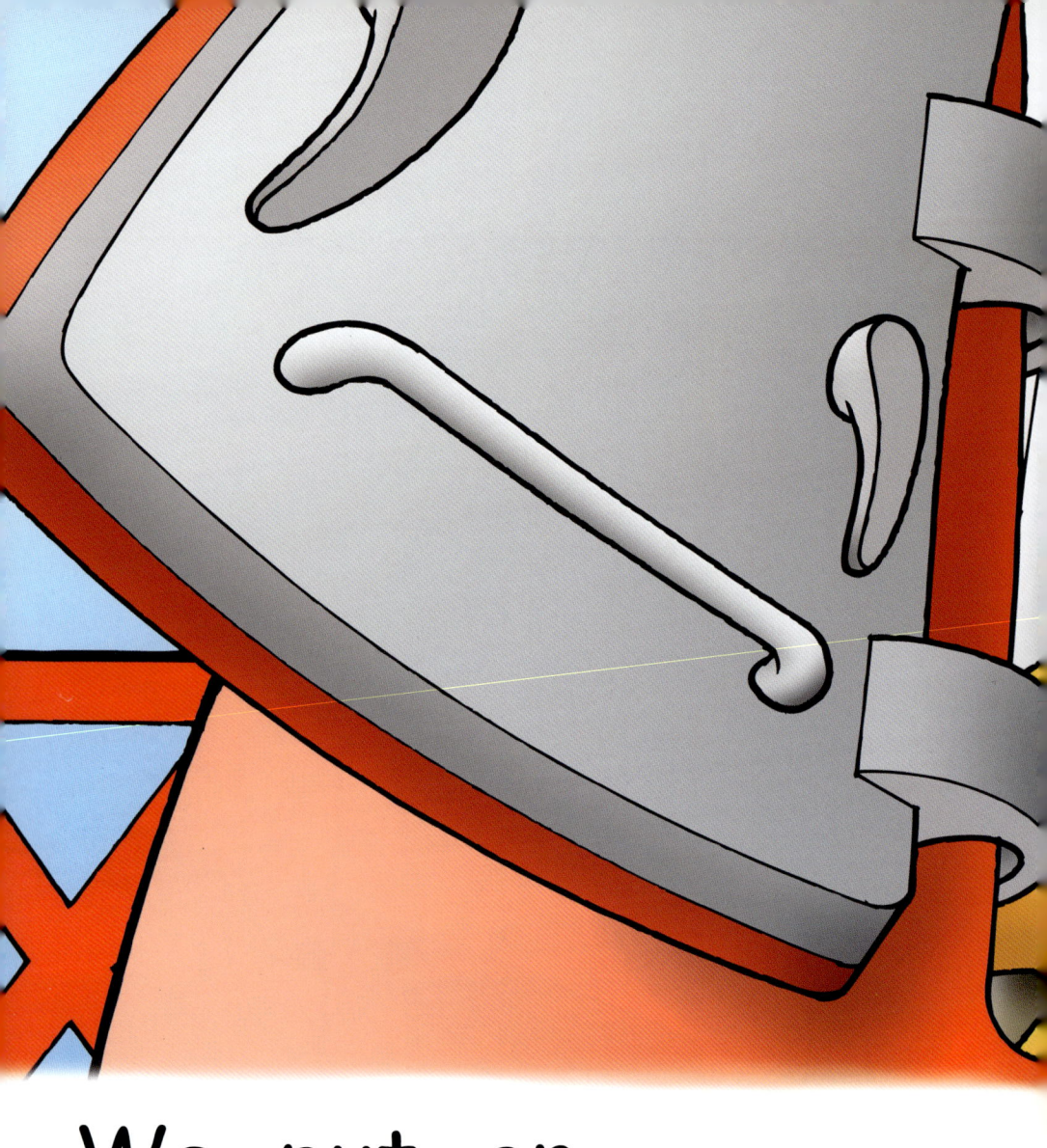

We put on
our safety belts.

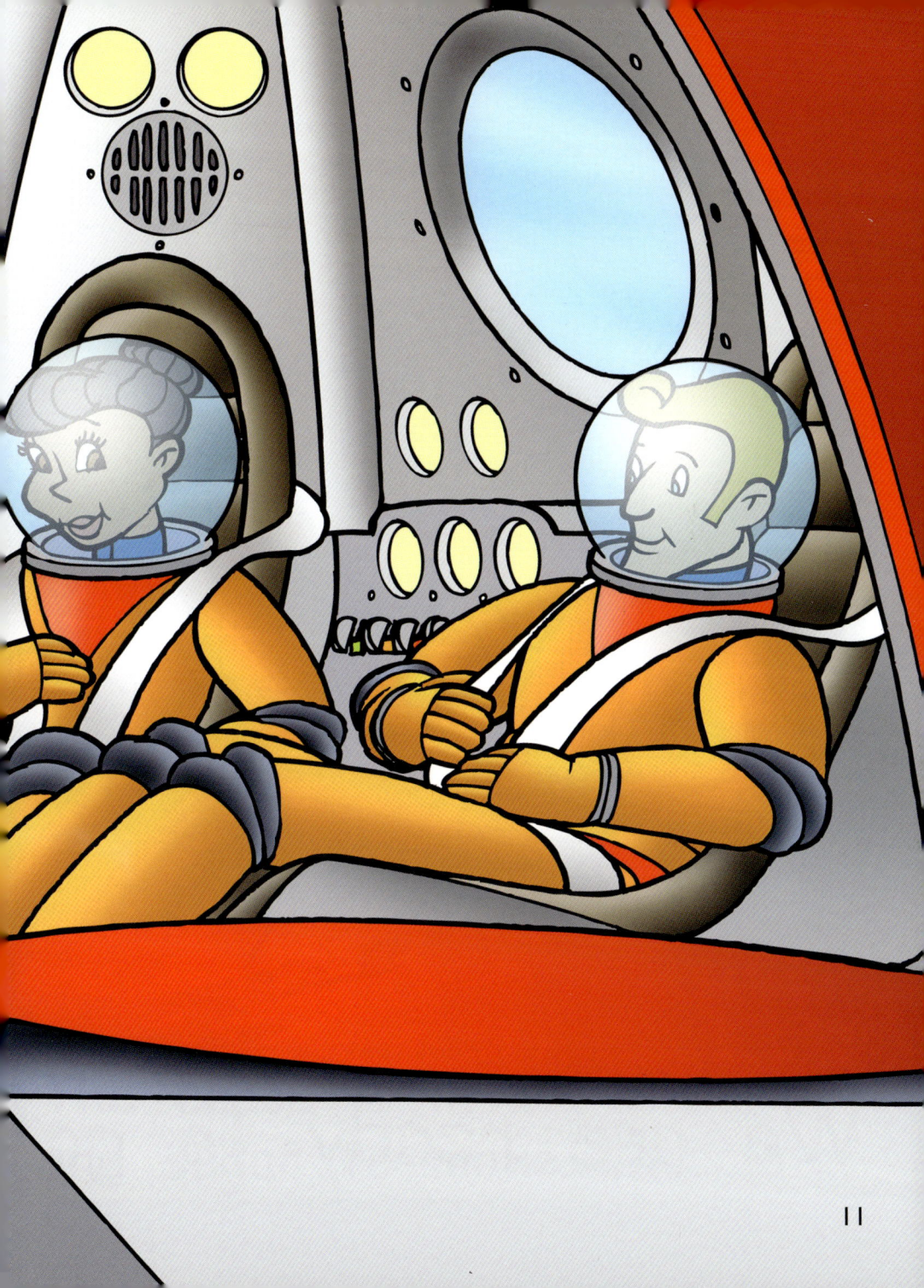

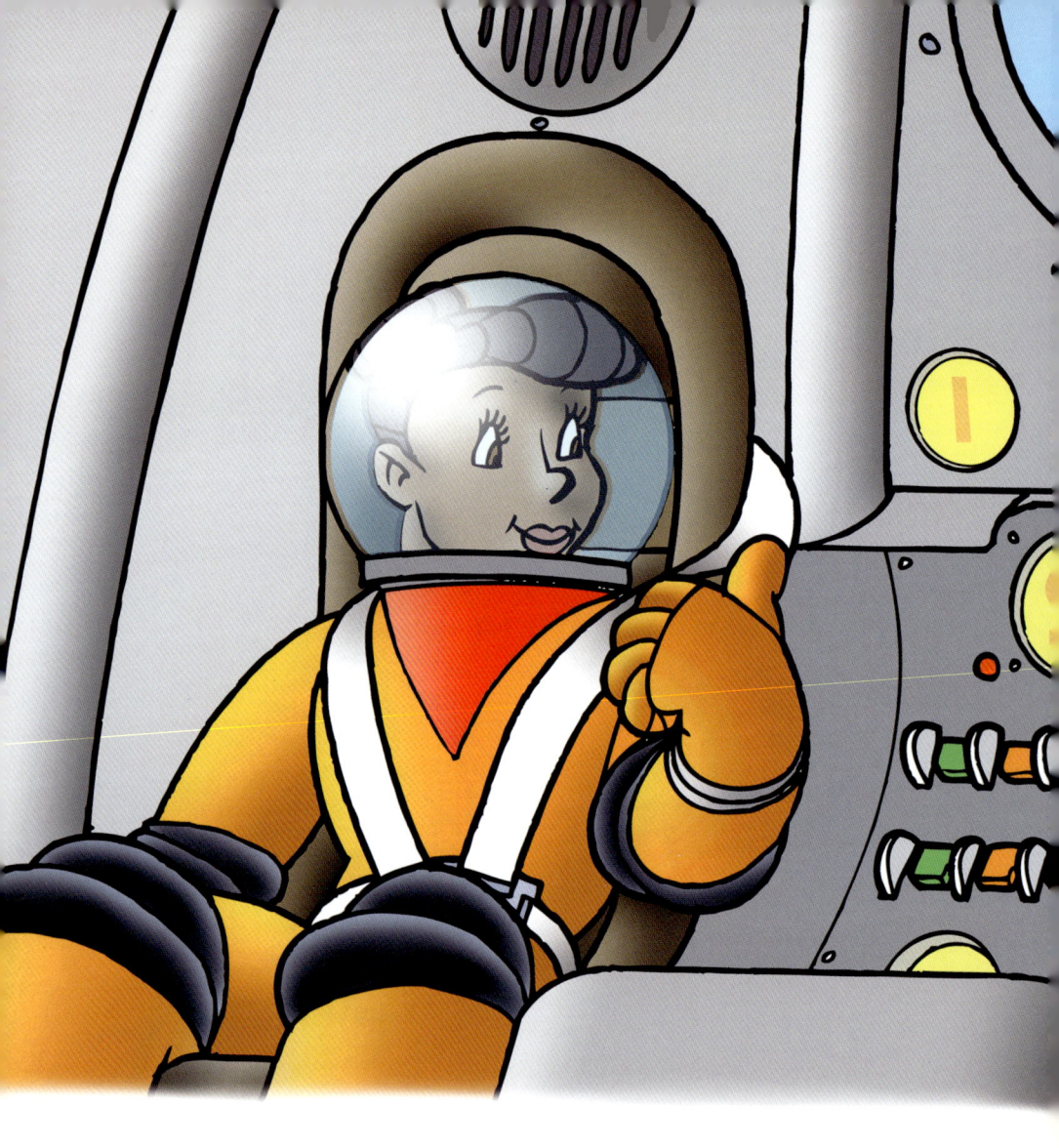

We are ready to go.

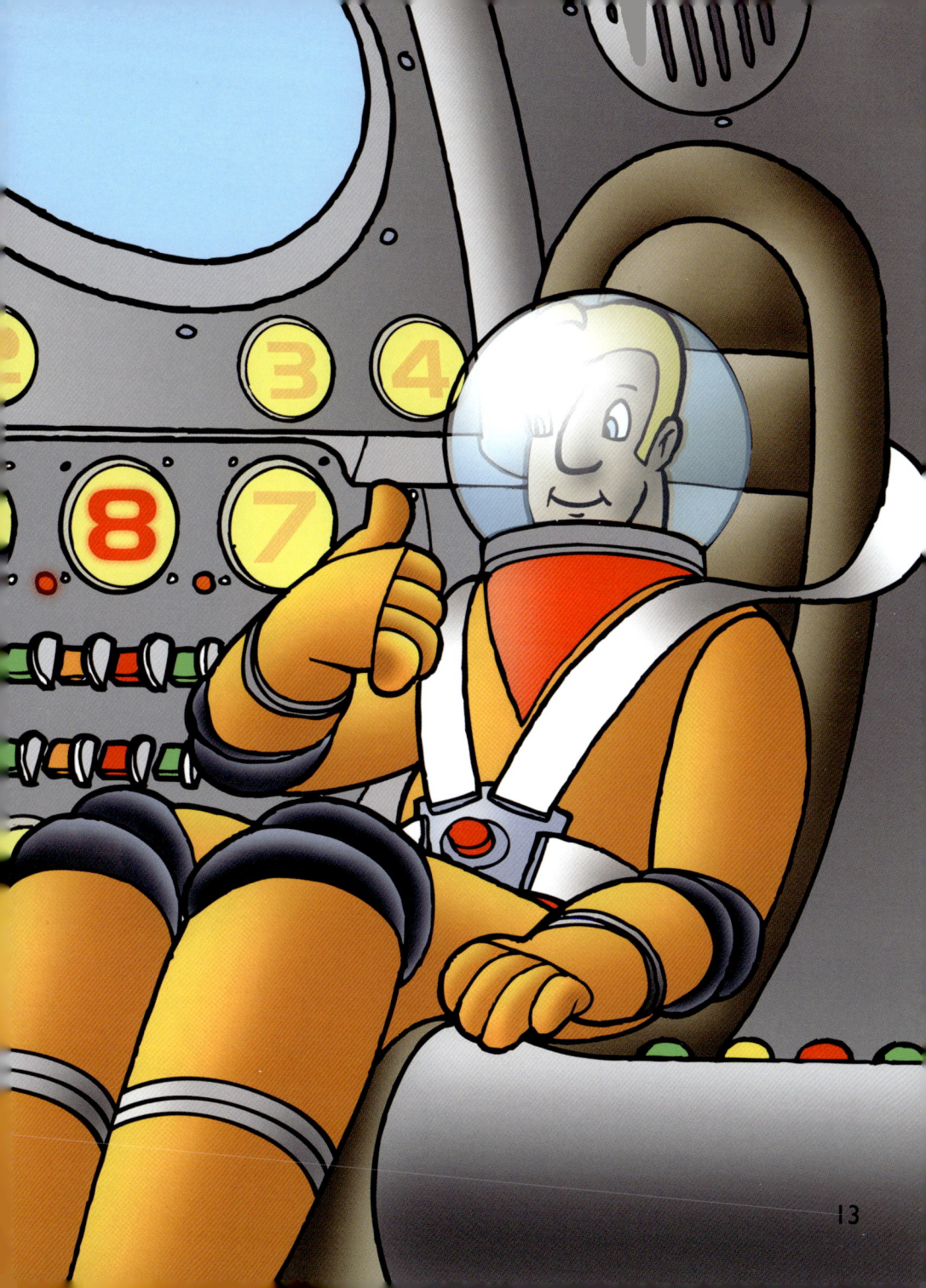

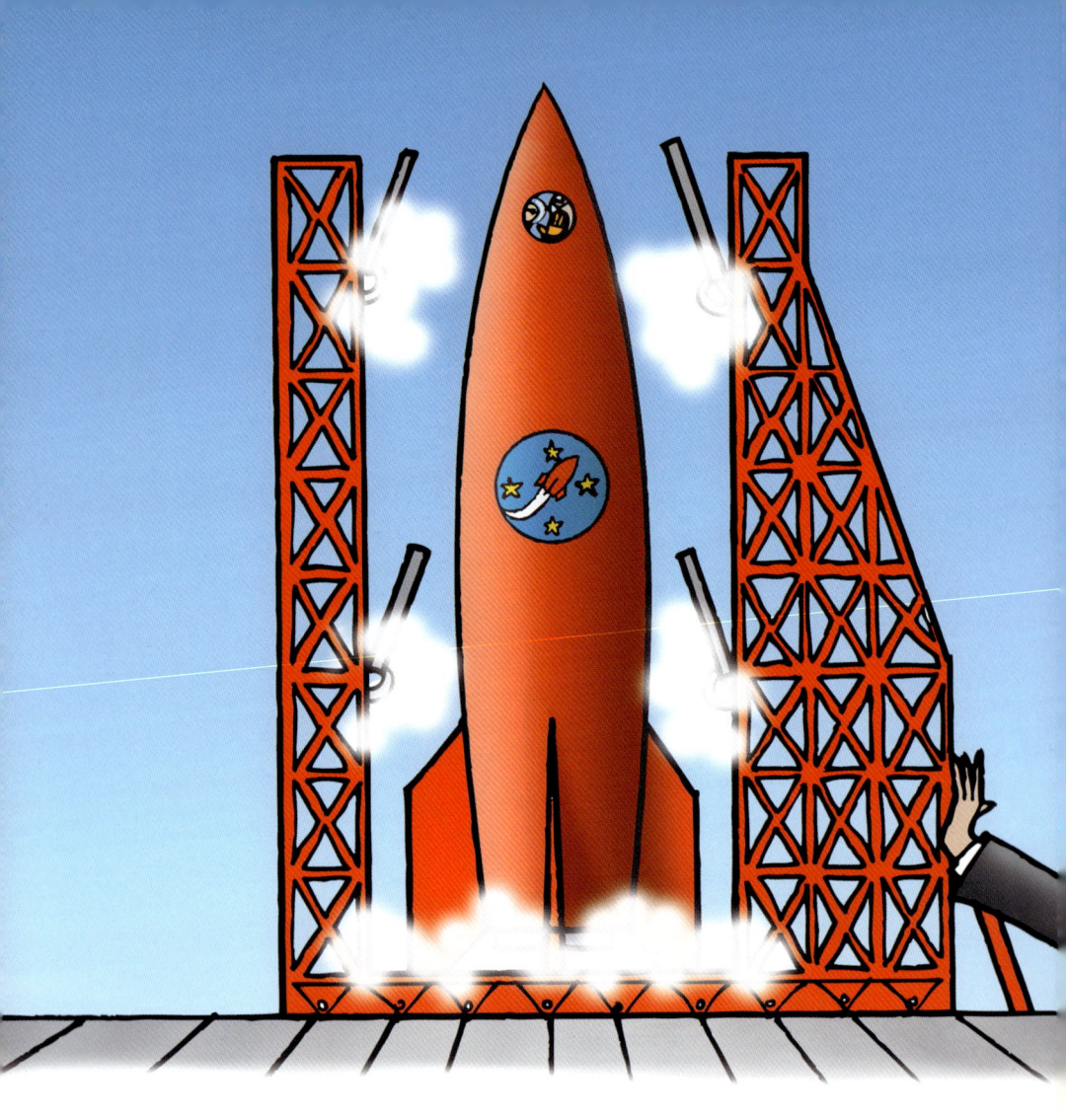

Ready! 10 9 8 7 6 5 4 3 2 1...

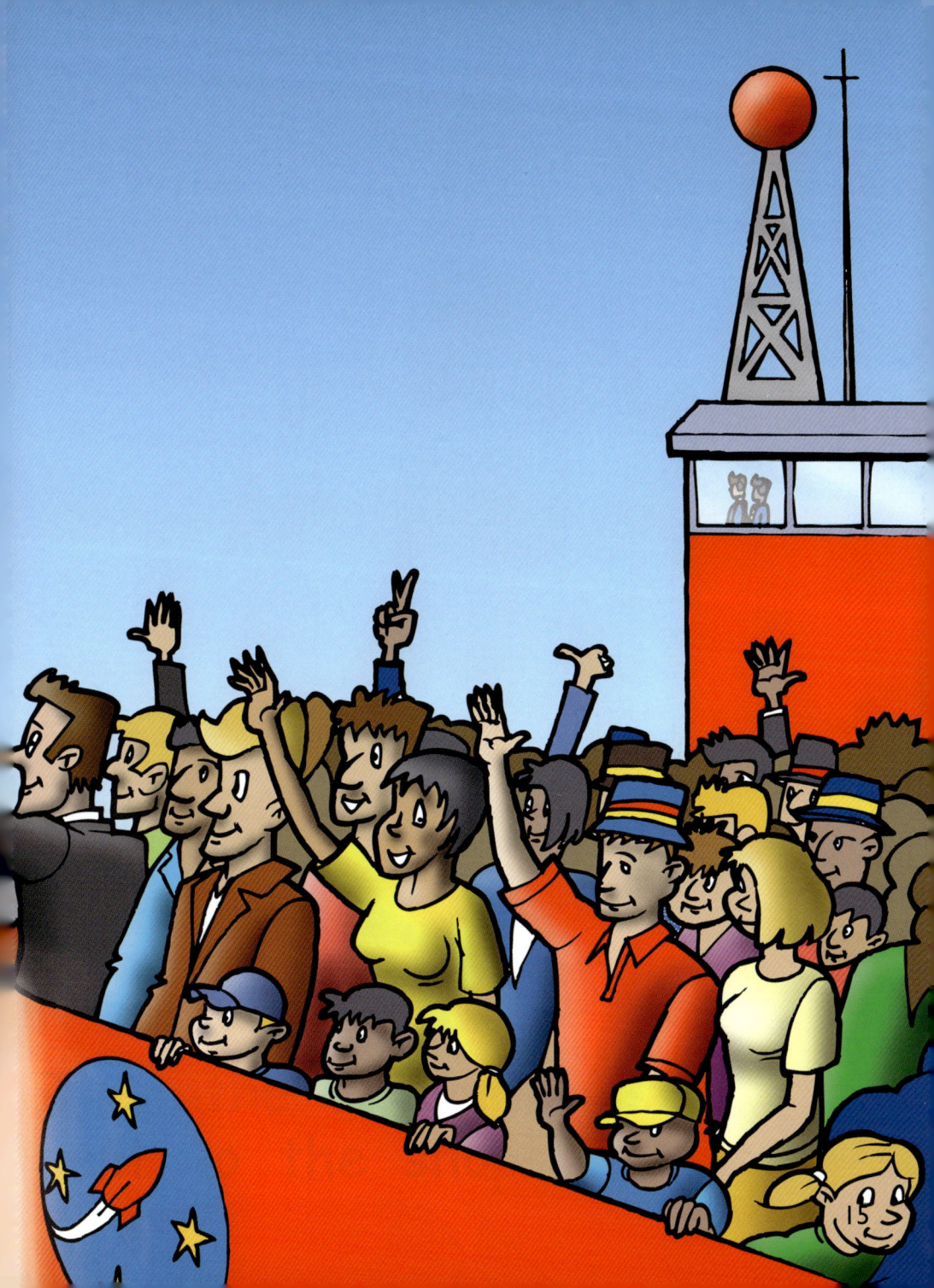

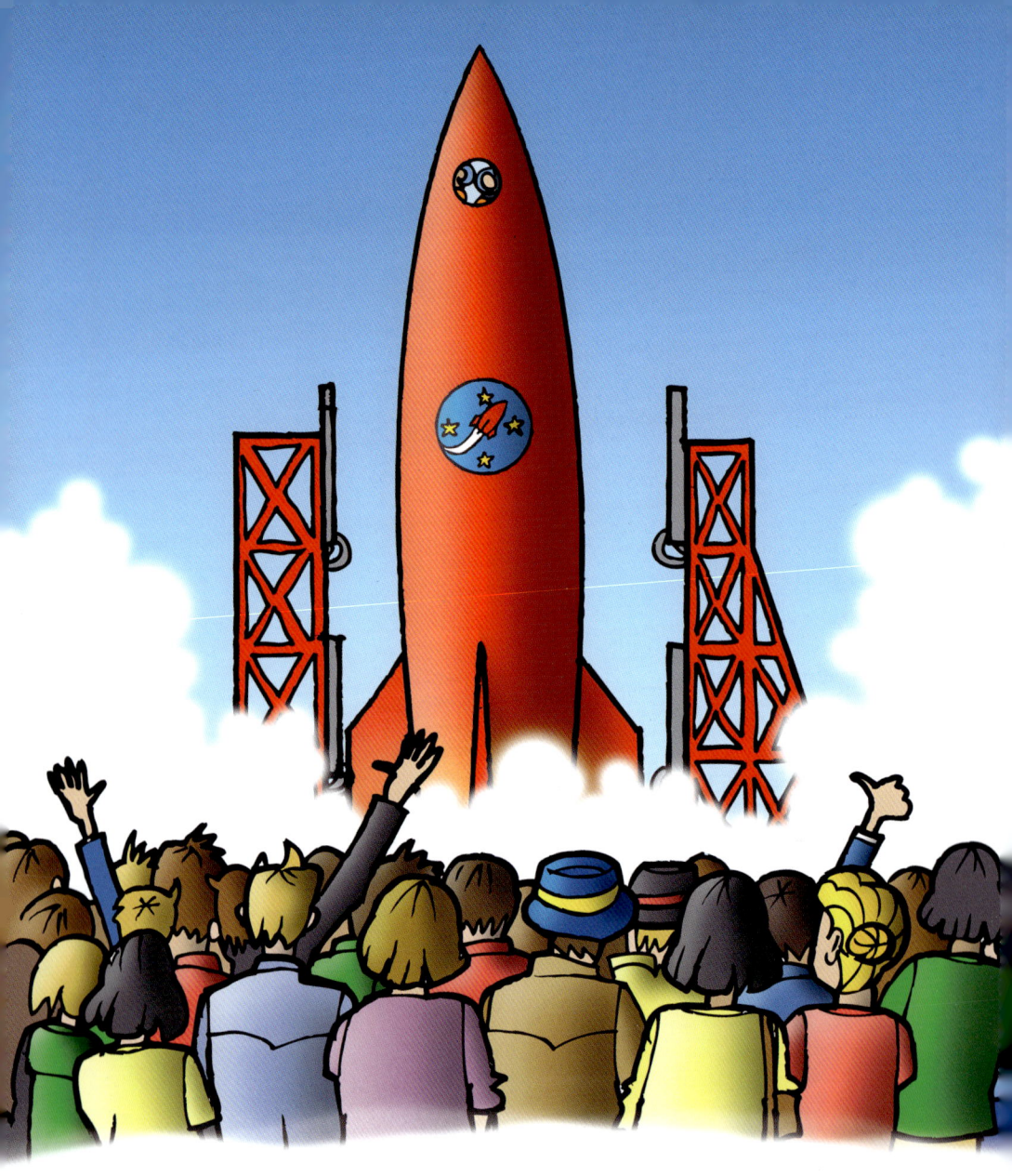

Lift off!